Mr. Putter & Tabby
Make a Wish

CYNTHIA RYLANT

Mr. Putter & Tabby
Make a Wish

Illustrated by
ARTHUR HOWARD

Harcourt, Inc.

Orlando Austin New York San Diego Toronto London

For Sarah and Audrey, with love
— C. R.

2260384

Text copyright © 2005 by Cynthia Rylant
Illustrations copyright © 2005 by Arthur Howard

www.HarcourtBooks.com

Library of Congress Cataloging-in-Publication Data
Rylant, Cynthia.
Mr. Putter & Tabby make a wish/Cynthia Rylant;
illustrated by Arthur Howard.
p. cm.
Summary: Mr. Putter thinks he is too old to celebrate his birthday,
but when he remembers some of his past birthdays, he changes his mind.
[1. Birthdays—Fiction. 2. Old age—Fiction. 3. Neighbors—Fiction.
4. Cats—Fiction.] I. Title: Mr. Putter and Tabby make a wish.
II. Title: Mr. Putter & Tabby make a wish. III. Howard, Arthur, ill. IV. Title.
PZ7.R982Msg 2005
[E]—dc22 2004010983
ISBN 0-15-202426-3

Manufactured in China

First edition

A C E G H F D B

1

Good Heavens!

It was a beautiful morning.
Mr. Putter and his fine cat, Tabby,
were eating raisin crumpets and apple jam
and reading the morning paper.

Mr. Putter looked at the date of
the paper: October 2.
"Good heavens, Tabby!" said Mr. Putter.
"It's my birthday!"

Tabby looked at Mr. Putter and purred.
She was a little messy from apple jam.
But she was glad it was Mr. Putter's birthday,
if birthdays meant apple jam.

Mr. Putter put the paper down
and began to think.
He thought of all his many birthdays—
especially those when he was a boy.

He had *loved* birthdays then.

He always got a really good present,

like a scooter or a model plane kit.

He got a cake with candles.

He got balloons.

He got company.

Birthdays were perfect days.

But now Mr. Putter was old.

Too old for scooters and model plane kits.

Too old for balloons.

Too old for a cake with candles.

(He'd need a fire hose to put them out.)

Mr. Putter was just too old for a birthday.

He would not think about it.

He would not think about cake

or candles

or balloons

or model plane kits.

He would enjoy his breakfast
with Tabby instead.
"More jam, Tabby?" asked Mr. Putter.
Tabby purred.
Jam was nice.
Jam was fine.
Mr. Putter would just have more jam.

2

Can You Wait?

Mr. Putter couldn't help it.
He wanted more than jam for his birthday.
"I am too old for birthdays, Tabby,"
said Mr. Putter.
"But I want one anyway."

Mr. Putter decided he could at least
have some company.
He would invite his neighbor Mrs. Teaberry
and her good dog, Zeke, to tea.

Mr. Putter called Mrs. Teaberry.

He told her it was his birthday.
He invited her to tea.

"Wonderful!" said Mrs. Teaberry.
"But first I have to do the dishes.
Can you wait?"
Mr. Putter said he could wait.

He finished reading the paper.

Mrs. Teaberry phoned.

"I have to curl my hair," she said.

"Can you wait?"

Mr. Putter said he could wait.

He took a little snooze.

Mrs. Teaberry phoned.

"I have to unclog the tub," she said.

"Can you wait?"

Mr. Putter said he could wait.

He read a book.

Mrs. Teaberry phoned.

"I have to find Zeke's ball," she said.

"Can you wait?"

Mr. Putter said he could wait.

He clipped his nails.

Mrs. Teaberry phoned.

"I'll be there soon," she said.

"Can you wait?"

Mr. Putter wanted to say, "NO."

Mr. Putter wanted to say,

"It's my birthday and I CAN'T WAIT!"

But Mr. Putter was nice.

He said he could wait.

(Even though he didn't want to.)

Mr. Putter was getting older by the minute.

Soon it would be *tomorrow.*

And tomorrow was *somebody else's*

birthday!

Mr. Putter looked at Tabby, who was curled
up in a bowl.
"So far, this is a very strange birthday,"
Mr. Putter said to Tabby.

3

Finally

Mr. Putter thought Mrs. Teaberry and Zeke
would *never* come to tea.
He thought he would have to wait *forever*.
He thought he would be waiting
until his *next* birthday.

But finally the doorbell rang.

Mr. Putter opened the door.

"SURPRISE!"

It was Mrs. Teaberry and Zeke.

And Mrs. Teaberry was carrying

an ENORMOUS cake loaded with

DOZENS of candles.

Zeke had a present around his neck.

And balloons on his tail.

"I had to make you wait," said
Mrs. Teaberry, "so I could bake a cake."

Mr. Putter looked at all the candles.
"I'll need a fire hose
to put those out," he said.

When tea was served and he had
opened his present (a model plane kit!),

Mr. Putter blew out ALL of his candles.
It took five big breaths (plus some help
from Mrs. Teaberry's hat).
But he got them out.

"Did you make a wish?" asked Mrs. Teaberry.
Mr. Putter looked at Tabby
and at Mrs. Teaberry and at Zeke.

And he couldn't think of anything
to wish for.
He had everything.
(Even a model plane kit.)

Mr. Putter and Tabby and
Mrs. Teaberry and Zeke ate cake
for days and days.

And Mr. Putter built his model
plane *almost* perfectly.
(He just got a little mixed up
on the tail.)
It had been such a wonderful birthday.
Of all the birthdays in Mr. Putter's
long life, this one really had been …

WORTH THE WAIT!

The illustrations in this book were done in pencil,
watercolor, and gouache on 250-gram cotton rag paper.
The display type was set in Artcraft.
The text type was set in Berkley Old Style Book.
Color separations by Bright Arts Ltd., Hong Kong
Manufactured by South China Printing Company, Ltd., China
This book was printed on totally chlorine-free Stora Enso Matte paper.
Production supervision by Ginger Boyer
Designed by Arthur Howard and Scott Piehl